PUBLISHED BY COLOUR LIBRARY BOOKS LTD
GODALMING, SURREY, ENGLAND
© 1988 PETER HADDOCK LTD
BRIDLINGTON, ENGLAND
Printed in Italy
ISBN 0 7105 0344 X

GOLDILOCKS
and
The Three Bears

Retold & Illustrated by John Patience

COLOUR LIBRARY BOOKS

Once upon a time there was a little girl called Goldilocks who lived on the edge of a great forest. She was called Goldilocks because she had very beautiful curly blond hair which gleamed like gold in the sunlight. But although Goldilocks looked so pretty she could sometimes be very naughty. Every day as Goldilocks went out to play, her mother would remind her: ''Now Goldilocks, you may go and play in the meadow, but don't go into the wood, or you will get lost.''

One morning Goldilocks began to grow tired of playing on the swing in the meadow. She couldn't catch any minnows in the stream and even her favourite doll seemed boring. ''I know,'' said Goldilocks to herself, ''I'll go exploring in the forest!'' She glanced back at the house to make sure her mother wasn't watching, then off she ran across the meadow and into the forest.

Goldilocks wandered deeper and deeper into the forest until, at last, she became completely lost. The trees began to appear menacing, she imagined she could see faces in them, peering down at her; and once she thought she heard a deep growling noise like the sound of a wild animal. She felt very frightened and was about to cry when, to her surprise, she saw a strange little cottage amongst the trees. It was thatched with fur! Goldilocks tapped on the door but there was no answer. Then she peeped in through an open window. There was no one home so Goldilocks climbed inside for a look around.

Inside the cottage a log fire was burning brightly and a table was laid for breakfast with three bowls of steaming porridge. It smelled delicious and Goldilocks suddenly realised how hungry she was. "I'll just try a little to see how it tastes," she said. First she tried the largest bowl, but it was too salty. Next she tried the middle-sized bowl, but it was too sweet. Finally she tried the little bowl. "That's just right," she cried and she ate it all up.

Round the fireside were three chairs. Feeling tired, Goldilocks decided to sit down. First she tried the big chair, but it was very uncomfortable. Next she tried the middle-sized chair, but that was no better. Then she tried the little chair, but it was too small and broke into pieces.

In the corner of the room was a staircase and Goldilocks climbed up to see what was at the top. There she found a bedroom with three beds in it — and of course, one was very big, one was middle-sized and one was small. She tried each bed in turn. The large one was too hard, the middle-sized one was too soft, but the little one was just right, and Goldilocks soon fell fast asleep.

Goldilocks would not have slept so peacefully if she had known that the cottage belonged to three bears, and at that moment they were coming down the wood-land path on their way home. Father bear and baby bear had been collecting fire-wood, and mother bear had collected a

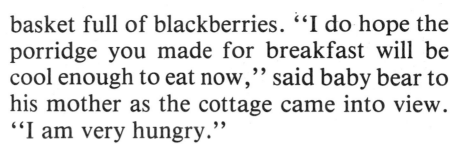

basket full of blackberries. "I do hope the porridge you made for breakfast will be cool enough to eat now," said baby bear to his mother as the cottage came into view. "I am very hungry."

As soon as they got into the house, the three bears went to the table to eat up their porridge. "Somebody," growled father bear in his big gruff voice, "Somebody has been eating my porridge." "Somebody," said mother bear in her medium-sized voice, "Somebody has been eating my porridge too." "And somebody has been eating my porridge, and eaten it all up!" cried baby bear in his baby-sized voice.

Then father bear noticed that the pipe he had left on his chair had been brushed off onto the floor. "Who's been sitting in my chair?" he roared in his great big voice.

"Who's been sitting in my chair?" said mother bear in her medium-sized voice. "And who's been sitting in my chair and broken it all to pieces?" cried poor little baby bear in his tiny little voice.

"Look, someone has left muddy footprints," growled father bear. "They go all the way up the stairs."

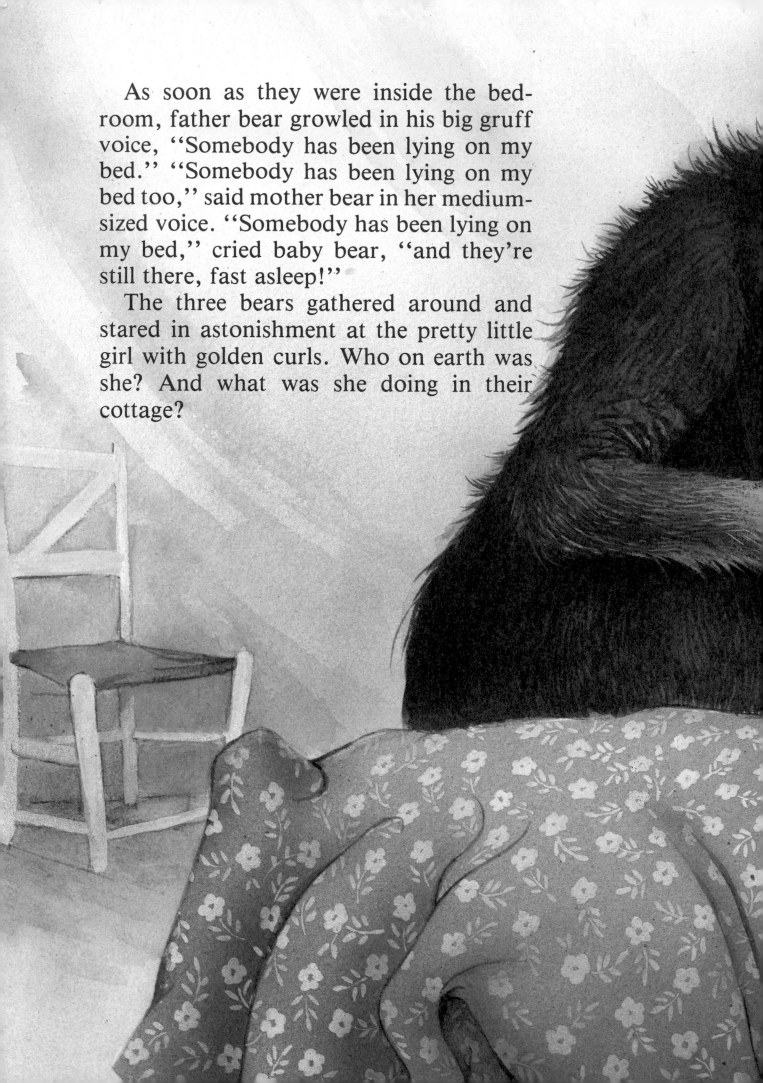

As soon as they were inside the bedroom, father bear growled in his big gruff voice, "Somebody has been lying on my bed." "Somebody has been lying on my bed too," said mother bear in her medium-sized voice. "Somebody has been lying on my bed," cried baby bear, "and they're still there, fast asleep!"

The three bears gathered around and stared in astonishment at the pretty little girl with golden curls. Who on earth was she? And what was she doing in their cottage?

Goldilocks woke up with a start and rubbed her eyes. She thought that the three bears were part of her dream, so she pinched herself hard, but the bears did not disappear. Now she was very frightened. "Goodness me, you're real!" she cried and, jumping out of bed, she ran down the stairs and out through the front door.

On and on she ran, not stopping for breath until at last she reached the edge of the forest and saw her own house, with her mother waiting on the doorstep for her. And she never went exploring in the forest again!